PLAYGROUND FUN

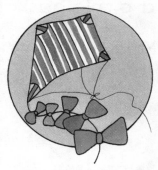

Written by
Sarah Toast

Cover illustrated by
Eddie Young

Interior illustrated by
Joe Veno

Louis Weber, C.E.O.
Publications International, Ltd.
7373 North Cicero Avenue
Lincolnwood, Illinois 60646

Permission is never granted for commercial purposes.

Manufactured in U.S.A.

8 7 6 5 4 3 2 1

ISBN: 0-7853-1076-2

PUBLICATIONS INTERNATIONAL, LTD.
Little Rainbow is a trademark of Publications International, Ltd.

Maria's dad is taking Maria and her two best friends to the new city park for the whole day. Maria and her dad pack lunch in a picnic basket. They bring along everything they'll need.

Nick and Nora are waiting at the entrance to the park. "Hurry, Maria!" calls Nora. "There's so much to do!"

"Let's go to the playground first," says Nick.

First they head for Fort Fun. Nick climbs a tall post all the way to the top. Nora balances on the tunnels. Maria waits for her turn on the rope swing.

They try the slide, swings, and teeter-totter. Then they go back to Fort Fun to climb and swing some more. Maria's dad looks for a picnic spot.

Next Maria's dad suggests going over to the duck pond. Everyone kneels at the edge of the pond to watch the mother duck and her three ducklings.

They try the slide, swings, and teeter-totter. Then they go back to Fort Fun to climb and swing some more. Maria's dad looks for a picnic spot.

Next Maria's dad suggests going over to the duck pond. Everyone kneels at the edge of the pond to watch the mother duck and her three ducklings.

Maria sees a frog and a turtle among the cattails growing in the pond. "It is nice that these animals have a good home in the city," she says.

"Now let's go to a different kind of pond," says Maria's dad. The children dash to the wading pool. In the middle of the wading pool is a stone fountain spouting water.

Maria's dad takes off his shoes to wade in the water with Maria, Nick, and Nora. "You look just like a big kid, Dad!" grins Maria.

"Let's go see more animals," says Nora.
She leads the way to the petting zoo.

The children feed some cows and
baby goats, and they even get to see a
llama up close. They wish they could stay
longer but Nick's tummy starts growling.

"You sound like you have a lion in your tummy, Nick!" says Maria's dad.

"I'm getting sort of hungry," says Nick.

"So are we!" say everyone else at once. They pick a nice spot for lunch. Nora spreads the mat. Nick sets out the sandwiches. Maria pours the juice, and her dad puts the fruit on a plate.

While they are eating lunch, Maria says, "Everywhere we've gone in the park today, a bluebird has been gathering twigs and leaves."

"Keep your eyes peeled," says her dad. "Maybe you'll see her nest."

After lunch they tidy up the picnic area.
Maria leaves a bread crust for the busy
bluebird. "Who would like to play a
game of baseball?" she asks. "I heard
there's a baseball diamond here."

They get to the diamond just as a game begins. Maria, Nick, and Nora have fun playing on different teams. Nick turns out to be a pretty good pitcher. Nora makes a home run. Maria catches a high fly ball.

Beyond the baseball diamond is a hill. It is breezy on the hilltop and there aren't many trees. It is the perfect place to fly kites.

"Let's go fly kites!" says Nora.

Park workers are handing kites to all the kids. The workers show how to let out the string so their kites can fly higher and higher in the sky. They explain how tails keep their kites from spinning around and crashing to the ground.

From the hilltop Maria, Nick, and
Nora can see people gathering below
to watch a show.

"Let's go watch," says Nick. They hurry
so they can get a good spot in the grass.

When they get there and sit down, a
man is setting up a little puppet theater.
He blows on a horn to start the show.
Then he makes his puppets perform a
funny play.

"We had a busy day, but not as busy as the bluebird's," says Maria. "Her nest is in this tree! It is the first new nest in our new park."